For Richard, Toby, and Sam.

What would I do without you?

— M. R.

Henry Holt and Company, *Publishers since 1866*
175 Fifth Avenue, New York, New York 10010
mackids.com

Henry Holt® is a registered trademark of Macmillan Publishing Group, LLC.
Copyright © 2017 by Maggie Rudy

Library of Congress Cataloging-in-Publication Data
Names: Rudy, Maggie, author, illustrator.
Title: City mouse, country mouse / Maggie Rudy.
Description: First edition. | New York : Henry Holt and Company, 2017. | Summary: City
mouse William Gray and country mouse Tansy become good friends who enjoy visiting each
other in the country and the city, but they miss each other when they are apart—is there a
way for them to meet halfway without giving up the city and country lives they love?
Identifiers: LCCN 2016050983 | ISBN 9781627796163 (hardcover)
Subjects: | CYAC: City and town life—Fiction. | Country life—Fiction. | Friendship—Fiction. |
Mice—Fiction.
Classification: LCC PZ7.1.R838 Ci 2017 | DDC [E]—dc23
LC record available at https://lccn.loc.gov/2016050983

Our books may be purchased in bulk for promotional, educational, or business use. Please
contact your local bookseller or the Macmillan Corporate and Premium Sales Department
at (800) 221-7945 ext. 5442 or by e-mail at MacmillanSpecialMarkets@macmillan.com.

First Edition—2017 / Designed by April Ward

The illustrations in this book were built, photographed, and edited by the artist.
The characters and sets are constructed from felt and found materials.
Lighting by Sarah Foster of Far & Away Productions.

Printed in China by Toppan Leefung Printing Ltd., Dongguan City, Guangdong Province
1 3 5 7 9 10 8 6 4 2

City Mouse, Country Mouse

Maggie Rudy

GODWINBOOKS

Henry Holt and Company New York

One summer day, Tansy Mouse was weeding her strawberry patch when she spotted a gray caterpiliar. "Got you, Mr. Fuzzy!" she said, and pounced.

"AYEEEEE!"

squeaked a voice.

"My tail!"

The two little mice gaped at each other.
Then they burst out laughing.

"Who are you?" said Tansy.
"I'm William Gray," said the mouse,
"and you scared the pants off me."
"I'm sorry!" said Tansy.
They sat down to talk
and eat strawberries.

There was so much to talk about! William was a city mouse, and Tansy had never been beyond the next field. He told her about the shops and cafés, the crowded sidewalks, the sounds and smells that filled the air.

"It's so exciting!" he said. "I could never live anywhere else!"

In the soft hum of the summer day, Tansy tried to imagine the city.

"The country is better," she said. "Come on—I'll show you." And she pulled Will to his feet and led him into her world.

Birds sang and bees buzzed, and the air was soft and sweet.

Tansy lifted her nose and sniffed. "Just *smell* the freshness!" she said.

All day long, the new friends wandered through the leafy green land, talking and laughing.
At last, Will looked up.

"The sun is getting low," he said. "I'd better be going."
"But I'll miss you!" said Tansy.
"I'll miss you, too," said Will.
"I miss you already!"
They looked sadly at each other. Then they shook paws, and he walked away.

But Will hadn't gone far before he turned back.

"Come with me!" he said.

"It'll be an adventure."

Tansy looked around her. The country would still be here when she got back.

"Let's go!" she said.

And they set off toward the city.

There was so much to see and do in the city!

Every day they
talked about their
dreams and planned
their adventures.
They were the
best of friends.

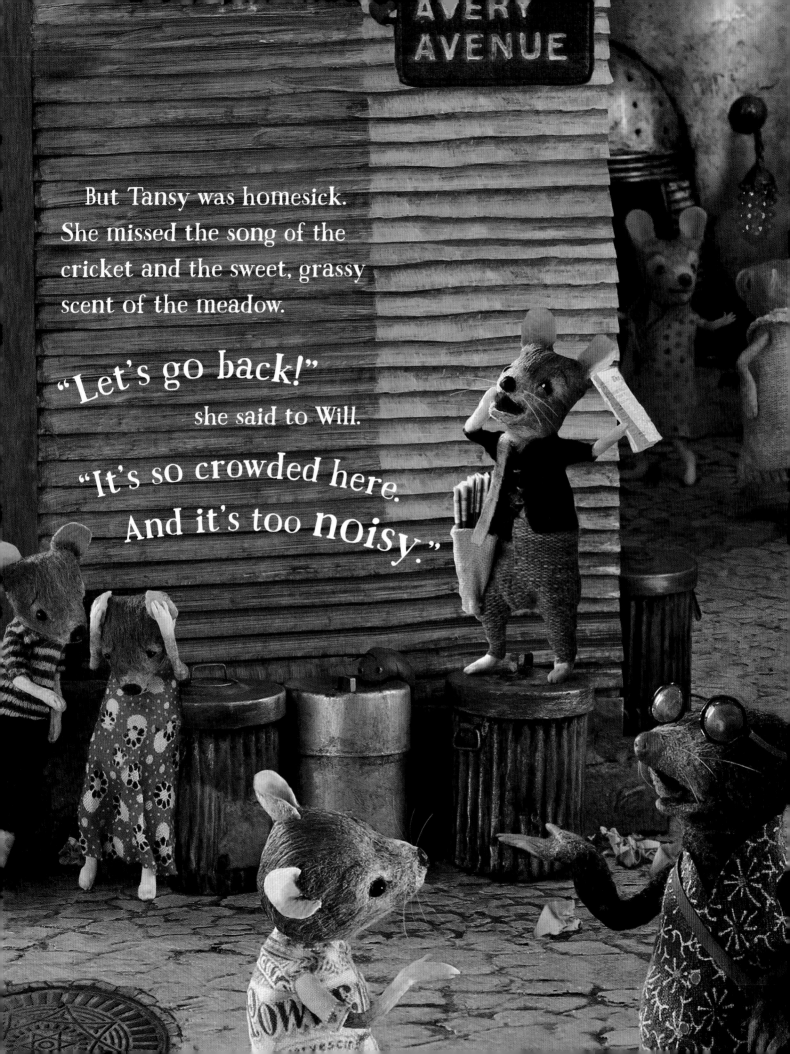

But Tansy was homesick. She missed the song of the cricket and the sweet, grassy scent of the meadow.

"Let's go back!" she said to Will.

"It's so crowded here. And it's too noisy."

"I could never leave the city!" said Will.
"It's exciting! The country is too quiet for me."

But Tansy packed her bag and left.

Back home in the country, Tansy felt the soft air and heard the sweet sounds she had longed for. But nothing seemed quite as wonderful without Will.

Alone in the city,
Will missed his friend.

The days passed, and the heat of summer gave way to chilly fall. The strawberry leaves shriveled in the frost, and Tansy made jam with the last berries.

Oh, how I wish I could share this with Will! she thought.

In the city, Will
looked for Tansy
in every face.

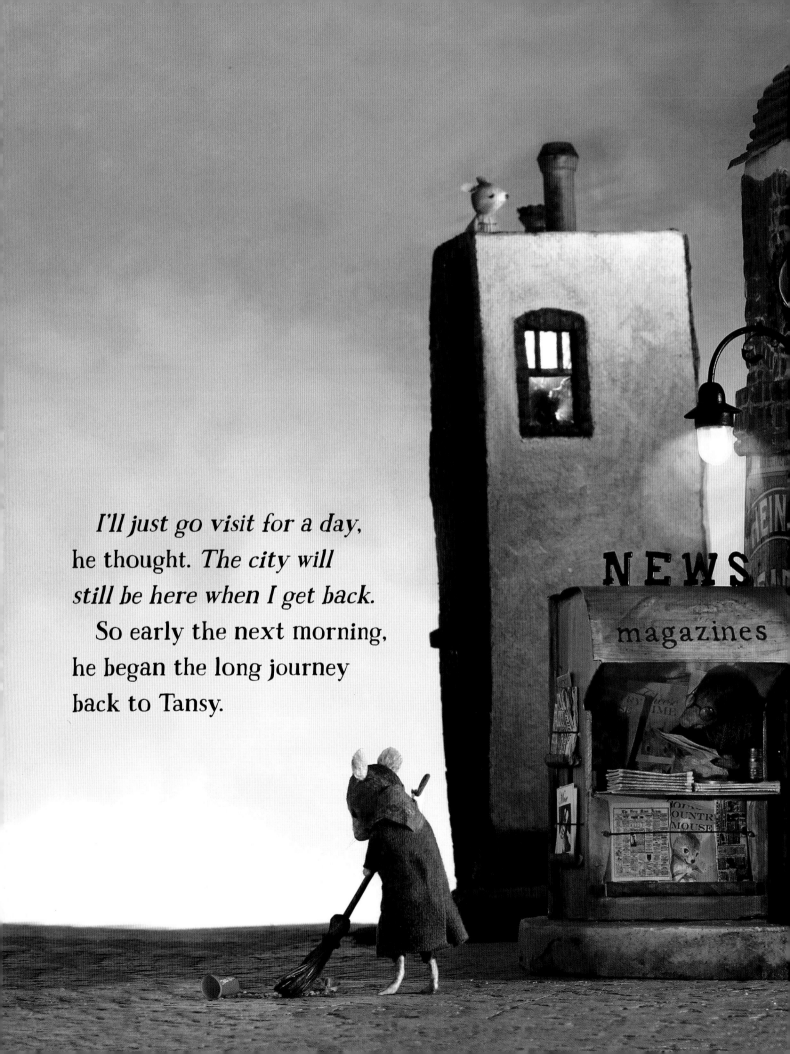

I'll just go visit for a day,
he thought. *The city will
still be here when I get back.*
So early the next morning,
he began the long journey
back to Tansy.

But when he was halfway there, whom did he see?

It was Tansy!

And she was on her way to visit him, too.

"I missed you!" they said at the same time,
and burst out laughing.

The two friends walked arm in arm through
the little one-street town and went into a café
for tea and cake.

"I like it here," said Tansy.
"I do, too," said Will. "It's not quite the country and not quite the city."
"It's in-between," said Tansy.

"Let's stay here!"

they both said at once.

So Tansy and Will settled into the halfway town.

It was just big enough for one grocery shop, one bookstore, and one café. It was close enough to the city that they could visit when Will got restless, and it was no farther to the country when Tansy longed for the sights and smells of home.

They lived right next door to
each other, and between their houses
they planted a strawberry patch.

They met there every morning to talk about
their dreams and plan their adventures.

And Tansy and Will, the best of friends, lived
mousily ever after.